For Phebe and Helen,
Julie and Joe,
pizza and movie nights.
—M.W.

Sally the pizza maker grows tomatoes in her community garden in the city. These tomatoes are for pizza.

Community Garden NEWS

Tomatoes

Wheat grown on
farms far away is milled
into flour and delivered to
Sally's pizzeria. This flour
is for pizza.

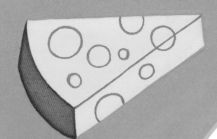
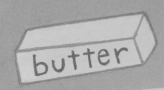

Milk is made into cheese
and sold in the shop next door.
This cheese is for pizza.

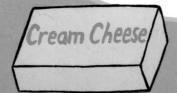

Sally opens her pizzeria in the morning. Hungry customers will be arriving soon. Orders will be coming in over the phone. But now it's time to make pizza.

Cut, chop, stir, and simmer.
There are good cooking smells
in the air. Sally makes her
tomato sauce.

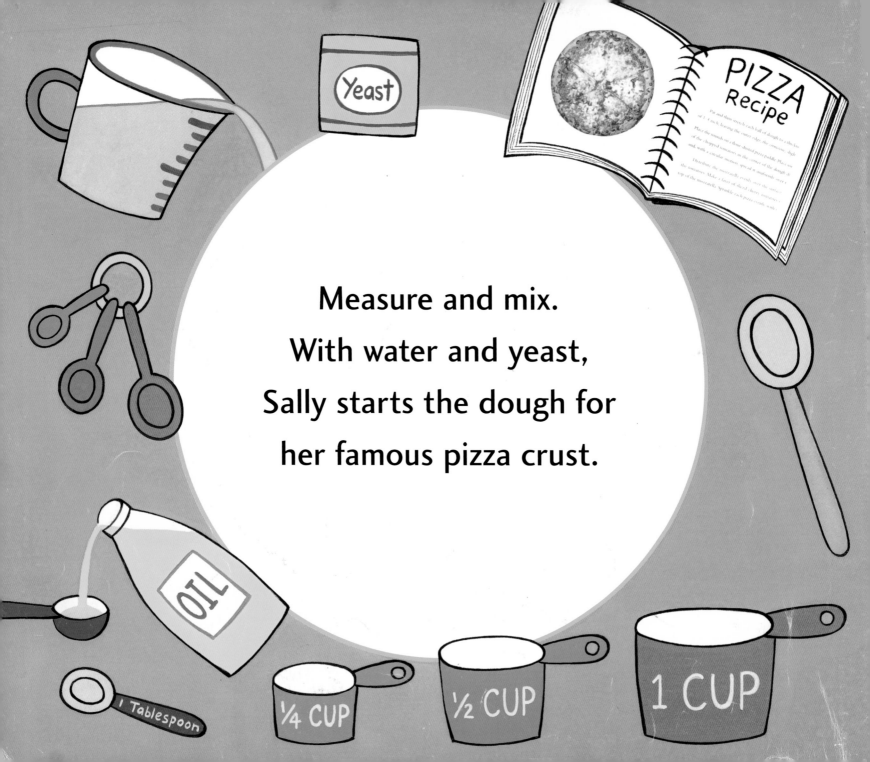

Measure and mix.
With water and yeast,
Sally starts the dough for
her famous pizza crust.

Push, pull, punch, and pound.
She kneads her stretchy
dough and leaves it to rise.

The dough is just right.
Sally rolls it and folds it
and rolls it again.
Whoosh—she twirls it
up into the air.

Now everything is ready to put together. First comes the pizza dough, then the tomato sauce. Then freshly grated cheese is sprinkled on top. Perfect!

MENU
Pizza Toppings:
Extra Cheese
Pepperoni
Mushrooms
Onion
Basil
Olive

Sally slides her pizza
into the hot oven. Mmm,
the pizzeria smells delicious
as the pizza bakes.

Out it comes, bubbly and hot. Quick—slice up the pizza and it's ready to eat!

Pop the pizza into a box. Some customers take theirs home to eat. Some have it delivered.

But eating pizza right
here at Sally's Pizzeria
is best of all.

The busy day is over and
the last customers have gone.
Now Sally and her little helper
can relax and enjoy a slice
themselves. How yummy!

Sally's Pizza Recipe

Makes 8 servings

The Dough

1 packet active dry yeast (1 tablespoon)
1 teaspoon sugar
1½ cups warm water
2 teaspoons salt
4½ cups flour

1. In a mixing bowl, dissolve the yeast and the sugar in the warm water.
2. Stir in one cup of the flour and the salt.
3. Add the next 3 cups of the flour, one cup at a time, mixing well until it is no longer sticky.
4. Knead the dough on a floured surface, until it is smooth and elastic, for 8–10 minutes, working in the remaining last ½ cup of flour.
5. Shape the dough into a ball and put it in a lightly oiled bowl, then cover with a cloth or plastic wrap.
6. Let it rise in a warm place for about an hour, until it has doubled in size.
7. Punch it down to get out air bubbles. Divide in two (or into the number of pizzas you want).
8. Pull and spread out the dough with your hands onto two lightly oiled 12-inch pizza pans or baking sheets.

The Topping

1 cup of your favorite tomato sauce
2 cups grated mozzarella cheese

1. Preheat oven to 400 degrees.
2. Spread ½ cup tomato sauce on each pizza.
3. *(Optional)* Arrange, on top, chopped vegetables of your choice, such as mushrooms, peppers, asparagus, broccoli, onions, herbs.
4. Sprinkle 1 cup grated mozzarella cheese on each pizza.
5. Bake in the oven for about 15 minutes or until the edges are golden brown.
6. Serve at once! *Buon appetito!*